THE GNELF ADVENTURES

THE QUEST FOR THE
CONIFER CROWN

Henry Hamilton-Turner

For my nephews, Leo and Matthew.

Inspired by all my wonderful childhood memories growing up on the Isle of Man.

Thank you to my parents, my sister, and friends who have helped me on this journey, and to Antonio, for his never-ending support and encouragement, and whose belief in me made this happen.

Contents

1

A Peculiar Sight

*T*he large grey rabbit stood up on its hind legs and looked out towards the empty playground. With a twitch of its nose and a flick of its tail, the rabbit did a perfect cartwheel across the vegetable patch.

Leo sat up, blinked and craned his neck. Rabbits cannot cartwheel, or so he thought. The glinting sunlight and the glare from the window were making it difficult for Leo to see down to his school's science garden. He shuffled his chair, careful not to draw Mrs. Shackleton's attention, and tilted his head to get a better view. Leo was convinced he had just seen a rabbit cartwheel across the cabbages, but he wanted to make sure.

Leo Dickens had been staring out of the classroom window, daydreaming about pirate adventures, when the rabbit had caught his eye. The rather large rabbit had shuffled along the vegetable patch, rather than hopping, which Leo thought was slightly odd as he had never seen a rabbit shuffle before, but that was nothing compared to the cartwheel. He must have been dreaming.

Leo shook his head and peered out of the window again. Some Year 1 children had entered the science garden and one of them was standing on a large, lonely rock. He didn't remember seeing the rock before, but where had the rabbit gone? Maybe there was a burrow nearby, or maybe his eyes had just been playing tricks on him. He was so sure he had seen a cartwheeling rabbit. The Year 1 children were squealing with glee and madly pulling up cabbages, carrots and radishes, so any rabbit would be long gone.

Leo's eyes drifted back to the front of the classroom and up to the large classroom clock above the interactive whiteboard; it always seemed to go so slowly. Tick, tick, tick; the pressure grew on the quivering hands. The ticking seemed to get louder and louder, but the hands seemed stuck. Tick, tick, tick, the pressure was building.

Any second now! Leo stared mesmerised, waiting for the final moment to come. Waiting, until... Tock! The second-hand suddenly sprang into life, lurching forward and leaping onto the next minute of the clock, before freezing, and the tick, tick, tick, started all over again. Leo sighed and slumped back in his chair.

It was the last day of term and Leo was desperate for school to finish. He daydreamed about the adventures he could have during the holiday. He wanted to be free, to take his bike out and cycle as fast as he could with the wind rushing against his face. Soon, he and his family would be at the beach, where perhaps, he would discover pirates smuggling gold or find real buried treasure. He started imagining the fame. He would be in the newspaper. Or better still, they might need to interview him, on television! He would become rich. Leo was puzzling whether he might be allowed to play himself in his own movie, when his thoughts were rudely interrupted.

"Leo Dickens! Are you with us?" Mrs. Shackleton asked him. "Please concentrate! What is 7 x 6?"

Quick as a flash all visions of stardom vanished. Leo tried to think clearly, he knew he was meant to know this, but before he could count up to 7 x 6 in his head, Mrs. Shackleton had moved on and asked someone else. She always seemed to know when he was doing his times tables in his head. His mind wandered back to buried treasure.

Leo could not concentrate in any of his lessons at school. He had disappointed his teacher in maths, and then managed to get most of his end-of-term spellings wrong. 'So, what!' he thought, he had far more important things to think about. It was very nearly the holidays.

Leo had a growing buzz of excitement that he got when he was about to do something he really loved. Tomorrow, he was going camping, to the seaside with his parents, but even better than that; his best friend, Matthew, was coming with him. Leo smiled at the thought of going away, they had not been camping for ages. Just one more sleep to go. Leo had to try and focus through one more lesson first, the last lesson of the day before the bell would ring and he would finally be free.

Sure enough, the history lesson dragged on, and after failing to concentrate through Mrs. Shackleton's description of Roman battle techniques, he was delighted to hear the school bell ring. At last, the lesson was over. Mrs. Shackleton switched off the interactive whiteboard and let them pack their schoolbags. Despite his own lack of interest in ancient Rome, Mrs. Shackleton was still Leo's favourite teacher, especially as she had brought in some homemade treacle toffee as an end of term treat. She stood at the front of the classroom and wished them all a wonderful holiday, reminding them to keep reading, before leading them out to the playground.

Leo said goodbye to Mrs. Shackleton and dashed across the playground to find his mother waiting by the flagpole. He was a slim boy and a fast runner, so he could dodge between the grown-ups very easily. His blond floppy hair flew out of his mottled blue eyes and he could feel the breeze on his freckled face. Why his mother always chose to stand there he never knew, as it was always the busiest part of the playground. The playground was packed with mums, dads, grannies and grandpas and there was an excitement in the air as children found their nattering grown-up.

"Come on Mum, let's go!" Leo said as he ran up to his mother, who was chatting to Alfie Garcia's father.

"Hello Freckle, in a minute. Have you had a good day? Alfie's father is telling me all about sunny Valencia," said Mrs. Dickens, "and we have to wait for Matthew anyway."

Leo hated being called 'Freckle', especially in front of others, but he had also forgotten that they were giving Matthew a lift home, and this cheered him up immensely. Matthew Masuda-Smith was the same age as Leo and they had been best friends for the last two years, ever since Matthew's family had moved to the same village that he lived in, Silverdale. His family had lived in the Middle East for a few years, but now they had moved back to England. Matthew and his family lived in the old stone house at the other end of the village, which backed onto a large forest called Muddletree Forest. Leo and Matthew would often cycle to each other's house, through the village, and get up to mischief. Leo loved playing at Matthew's house although they were still not allowed into Muddletree Forest alone. Apparently, it was "dangerous", according to Mrs. Masuda-Smith, and they might get lost. However, Leo and Matthew thought this was silly and they had recently made a secret pact that one day they would go and explore the forest by themselves.

As Leo stood in the playground waiting for Matthew, he glanced over to the science garden. He could see a few cabbages left over and an abandoned carrot on the pathway, but still no sign of that rabbit. Leo decided not to tell Matthew he thought he had seen a cartwheeling rabbit; he would just laugh at him.

Leo was still puzzling about it all when he felt a friendly nudge on his arm. He turned to see Matthew standing next to him, who was smiling from ear to ear. Matthew was a tall friendly boy with shiny black hair, brown eyes and a large grin which always showed off his perfect teeth. He was very easy-going and could speak fluent Japanese, which always impressed everyone. Matthew's parents had met in Japan when his father was a teacher there. They had moved to Dubai for a few years, before deciding to settle back in the United Kingdom, and Leo was very pleased they had chosen Silverdale. Matthew had joined Leo's class at the start of last year and they had been put next to each other. Mrs. Quayle, their class teacher last year, had wanted Leo to look after Matthew, and Leo had been delighted as lots

19

of children had wanted to be the new boy's best friend. Leo was quite shy to start with, but during their first maths lesson Matthew had leant over and helped him with his sums. Leo thought that was very cool and naturally, Leo had liked him ever since. In return, Leo would help Matthew with his French work and soon enough, the two of them had become inseparable, often giggling and distracting each other in class, much to Mrs Quayle's annoyance. This year, Leo and Matthew had been split up. Leo was put in Mrs. Shackleton's class, but Matthew had been put into Mrs. Moolai's class. However, they had remained best friends and last term they had shared an eighth birthday party, as Matthew's birthday was only five days after Leo's.

"Guess what Alfie did in class," Matthew said grinning, "He kept asking Mrs. Moolai questions about her two cats, and you know how much she loves talking about Tigger and Bruno. She was so distracted that she totally forgot to set us any holiday homework!"

Leo glanced at his mother and Alfie's father to see if they had heard what Matthew had said, but Mrs. Dickens was too busy hearing about Valencian paella. Leo smirked at Matthew, but then gasped as he suddenly realised Mrs. Shackleton had not given them any homework either. Brilliant!

"Quick!" he whispered to Matthew, "Mrs. Shackleton forgot too. Let's get out of here before one of them remembers." He turned around and yanked his mother's hand. "Come on!" he said pleadingly.

At that moment Alfie appeared at his father's side, so Leo took the opportunity to drag his mother across the playground towards the school gates. Leo and Matthew kept checking to see if Mrs. Shackleton or Mrs. Moolai would suddenly remember and come chasing after them. They reached the car and both boys breathed a huge sigh of relief. They all waved as they drove past Alfie and his father and soon the school was behind them. It was holiday time.

2

Cosy Nook Campsite

Leo woke up the next morning to see the sun streaming through his window and he could hear music playing on the radio downstairs. He started to drift back to sleep when he suddenly opened his eyes and sat up in bed. It was the holidays and today they were going camping. He jumped out of bed, pulled on any clothes he could find and ran downstairs into the kitchen, eager to get the day started. His mother was busy making some sandwiches for the journey and his father, who was reading the newspaper, looked up over the top of his reading glasses and stared at Leo.

"Good morning, Leo," he started, "What on earth are you wearing?" he then scoffed. Leo's younger sister

Isabella, or Issy as she was known, was already sitting at the table, and she giggled and pointed at Leo, staring through her mop of ginger hair.

Leo ignored his little sister, brushed his floppy hair out of his eyes and looked down. He realised he had pulled on his white school shirt and a pair of clown trousers from his dressing-up box. He did look a little strange.

"They are very comfortable thanks Dad," Leo said, pretending he didn't care, "What's for breakfast?" He sat down and stuck his tongue out at Issy, who had chocolate spread all over her face. Issy ignored Leo and instead slipped a bit of chocolate-coated toast under the table, where Rocket was waiting patiently, wagging her tail and licking her lips.

Rocket was a two-year-old dalmatian with gently flopping ears and big brown eyes. She had come from a litter of fourteen puppies, but she had chosen Leo's family because when they had gone to choose one of the puppies, she had trotted over to Mr. Dickens and laid her head against his leg, winning all their hearts. She had grown into a strong but slender dog, with soft white fur and she had a rocket-shaped black spot on her back, which was set apart from the other black spots. Naming her had been very easy and Rocket had quickly learnt that sitting next to Issy's chair was the most rewarding spot under the table.

"There are some croissants in the oven as a holiday treat," replied Leo's mother. "As soon as you have finished, go upstairs and get dressed properly so we can get going. Matthew will be here soon."

Leo wolfed down two buttery croissants covered with a generous portion of homemade bramble jam, followed by some apple juice, and then rushed back upstairs to change into some normal clothes. He did not want Matthew to see him looking weird. He brushed his teeth and finished packing the bag that his mum had helped him with the night before. He was zipping up the bag when he heard the doorbell ring. 'That must be Matthew,' he thought. He was so pleased that Matthew was coming. It meant he would be spared from having to do loads of really boring things with his mum and dad or having to play with Issy all the time. He and Matthew would take Rocket and go exploring and have real adventures together.

Leo heaved his bag downstairs and gave it to his father. He saw his mother and Mrs. Masuda-Smith chatting at the front door. Matthew, who was standing next to them, grinned and bounded over to Leo.

"Hi Leo," Matthew said enthusiastically, "This is so exciting! I can't wait! I've never been camping before."

"What? You've never been camping? Ever?" Leo was shocked.

"No not really," replied Matthew, "It was way too hot in the desert and there were scorpions and snakes. Although, that's just what mum said. I think it would have been cool!"

Leo thought that would have been very cool indeed. He wished he had lived in Dubai too, although he worried whether Rocket might have tried to eat the scorpions. He was just about to ask how big the scorpions were, when he heard his father shouting from outside. The car was packed and ready to go. Leo's mother checked that all the windows and doors were shut, before helping Issy with her seatbelt. When everyone was out of the house Leo's father turned on the burglar alarm and locked the front door. "Where's the dog?" asked Mr. Dickens, and to his dismay, he saw

Rocket was sitting between Leo's mother's legs in the front of the car.

"The boot's full!" she explained.

"Hmph! Just keep her still!" he said, rolling his eyes.

Matthew's mother leaned in the back of the car and gave the three children some strange-looking Japanese snacks for the journey.

"It's seaweed!" she said joyfully, much to Matthew's embarrassment.

The journey would take a couple of hours, but the boys didn't mind, they knew it would be worth the wait. Matthew's mother stood and waved them off, and soon they were driving out of Silverdale and heading towards the coast.

Trees, fields and hedgerows rolled past the windows endlessly and the seaweed snacks had not been very popular. Leo and Matthew were just beginning to wonder if the drive would ever finish when Leo's mother turned to face them and said smiling "Guess what! We're nearly there!"

The boys sat up eagerly and looked out of the window. The car had turned off the main road and they were now driving down a country lane towards a glimmering stretch of sea that sparkled in the distance. There were green fields stretching out on either side of the road with blackberry bushes and hawthorns running along the edges. Off to the side, they could see a line of trees that were the start of a large forest that spread over the hills beyond. It looked very similar to Muddletree Forest behind Matthew's house. As Leo stared into the darkness of the forest, he suddenly felt a little bit uneasy. He was not sure if he liked the look of shadows under the trees. They made him feel nervous, but he was not sure why. Then he noticed two large rabbits sitting at the edge of the forest. They looked just like the one he had seen in the science garden at school. The car turned a corner and when the rabbits came back into view, he realised they were not rabbits after all, but just two large rocks instead. Had he made the same mistake again? 'So weird,' he thought. He shook his head and decided that he was just being silly again.

"Hey Matthew, look over there," Leo said, "it reminds me of Muddletree Forest."

"Yeah, maybe we can explore this forest instead," whispered Matthew, "My mum's not here to stop us!"

They were interrupted by a howl of dismay from Mrs. Dickens who was furiously winding down the window whilst wrinkling her nose. "Who gave the dog chocolate?" she exclaimed. "Isabella, you know it's bad for dogs!" Soon all the windows had been rolled down to let fresh air in but Rocket just wagged her tail proudly.

Soon afterwards, they turned down a farm track, drove through an open gate and into a large grassy field, which had tents and campervans of every size and shape dotted along the stone walls. There was a washing block at the far end, and they had paused next to a little reception block that had whitewashed stone walls. Leo looked up to see an old sign hanging from the roof that said in bright blue letters "Cosy Nook Campsite." A rather jolly-looking woman came out and explained they could choose their pitch and then come back to check in.

Leo's father drove on slowly, avoiding the odd rabbit hole or mound, and stopped the car next to an empty pitch in a corner of the field. He said the tent would be more sheltered there and a bit more private. Leo and Matthew jumped out of the car, desperate to stretch their legs and to have a look around.

"Dad, please can we go and explore! Please!" begged Leo knowing full well that putting up the tent was the worst job ever, and always made his Dad cross.

Before Leo's father had a chance to say anything Mrs. Dickens replied instead.

"Yes boys, what a good idea! Go and explore a little bit, but don't go too far. Take Rocket with you." She then paused before adding "I think I had better go and check-in at reception. Issy, you come with me."

Leo glanced at his mother and thought that maybe she didn't want to help with the tent either, but without another word Leo tugged at Matthew's sleeve and they ran off towards a small wooden gate halfway along one of the old stone walls. Rocket lolloped after them.

The boys ran through the rickety gate and let it clatter shut behind them. They stood and looked down the little path, which led to the beach that opened out in front of them. The sides of the path were a little overgrown but the path itself had a layer of thick mossy grass that had obviously been well trodden and squashed down. The path wound its way down to the same glimmering sea that Leo had seen from the car.

"Come on, let's go and explore the beach!" shouted Leo enthusiastically.

The boys could not wait to get to the shore and leapt through the bouncy grass, laughing and shouting as they went. They soon emerged onto on a strip of beautiful shimmering sand that sloped gently downwards to some shiny pebbles and smooth seashells scattered along the shoreline, and the lazy waves that broke softly over them. The sea lay still and quiet and the odd ripple sparkled in the sunlight.

They looked up and down the beach. In one direction, at the far end, they could see some large, jagged rocks that looked like dragon's teeth. These rocks seemed to be protecting the steep cliffs behind them. Leo thought they looked quite dangerous but didn't want to say that to Matthew. He thought here might be some good shrimping pools, but he was not sure if it would be safe to explore them. In the other direction, the beach eventually narrowed until it disappeared into the start of the same dark forest that Leo had seen from the car. The one that had given him that strange, uneasy feeling. The forest rose from the beach and along a cliff, stretching as far as they could see.

33

"Which way should we go?" asked Matthew.

Leo looked up and down the beach and was not sure that he really wanted to go either way, and decided he would be braver tomorrow.

"Umm, I know," Leo said, "Let's go for a paddle in the sea!"

The boys kicked off their shoes and ran down to the water's edge. Rocket followed them leaping into the sea, frolicking in the shallows and barking at the tiny waves. They threw sticks for her to fetch and, as they splashed in the gentle surf, Leo was distracted by the jagged rocks and the dark forest. Would he and Matthew be able to explore them and why did he have a strange feeling about the forest? His mind drifted back to those two rocks that he had just mistaken for rabbits. How did he make the same mistake twice? Either way, Leo knew that he and Matthew would have to come back to the beach and take a closer look.

3

A Prisoner in Need

$\mathcal{T}$he first day passed by rather quickly. Thankfully, Leo's father had successfully put up the tent without any disasters, the sun had shone, and the boys had enjoyed playing at the campsite and down on the beach. They had been made to go shell-collecting with Issy, which she had been delighted about, but they decided it was a girl's activity and spent most of the time eyeing up potential skimming stones instead. They had barbequed burgers for dinner, and they all began to relax into the holiday.

On the second day another family took the pitch next to theirs, which Leo's parents muttered about. However, their smart red campervan was rather impressive and had won over Leo's father. They also had one child, a daughter called Rosalia, known as Rosie, who was the same age as Issy, and the two girls had quickly become best friends. This was great news for Leo and Matthew because it meant the girls would play games together, whilst the adults would be too busy chatting and playing cards to worry about what they were doing and where they were. This meant more time exploring.

It was the morning of the third day, and after a breakfast of toast and honey, Leo and Matthew wandered lazily down to the beach as usual. Issy made Rocket stay with her and Rosie, so they could have a tea party. During those first couple of days the boys had built sandcastles, played football, and pretended they were pirates on the high seas. Rocket had happily played the role of the shark, chasing them up and down the beach. They had held a stone skimming contest, which Leo was sure he would win, but Matthew had found the best stone on the beach. When Matthew won, Leo was frustrated and accused Matthew of cheating. He later apologised to Matthew and they had quickly become friends again. So, now they wanted something new to do.

"What do you want to do today?" asked Matthew. "We could go and explore those rocks over there," pointing up the beach, "or go that way and see what's in the forest?" he said, turning and pointing the other way down the beach. "Remember, my mum's not here to stop us!"

Leo had a choice to make. They could either go and explore the jagged rocks that he thought looked quite dangerous or go and explore the dark forest that had made him feel a little bit uneasy. Matthew said he didn't mind what they did, although Leo suspected he would prefer to go to the forest. Leo thought that the forest could not be any scarier than Muddletree Forest, so that seemed the best option. Although, he also remembered that Muddletree Forest had never given him funny feelings before.

"Ok, let's go that way," Leo said, pointing to the forest.

"Come on then, I'll race you!" shouted Matthew as he tore off down the beach. Leo loved a challenge and did not want to lose, so he sprinted after Matthew. The boys raced to the end of the beach, until they could go no further. They stood panting and laughing, trying to catch their breath. Here the shore narrowed and disappeared under the uneven and mossy ground leading up to the edge of the forest. The trees did not look quite so scary up close, and Leo's uneasiness started to disappear.

Leo also wanted to look brave in front of Matthew, so took a deep breath and said "Come on! Let's go in and see what we can find."

"Yeah," replied Matthew, "There could be all kinds of things that have been washed up from the sea. Maybe we'll find something cool."

"Or maybe we'll find a pirate's den with skeletons and treasure," laughed Leo as they stepped into the unknown forest.

The trees in the forest were tall and strong, and their leaves rustled in the sea breeze. There were a few different types of tree, but Leo recognised the sycamore trees with their helicopter seeds. Their leaves were all pock-marked white from the salt that had blown in from the sea. The sunlight dappled through the leaves and fell to the forest floor. Brambles and ferns grew in clusters and small birds chirruped and darted between the branches. Rhododendron bushes filled some of the gaps at the edge of the forest and often blocked the view in and out of the forest.

The two boys walked through the forest searching for lost items hiding on the forest floor. They found an old digital watch that had stopped working and one abandoned flip-flop. Leo was looking under a rhododendron bush when Matthew got his attention.

"Look up there!" he whispered, and Leo looked to where Matthew was pointing. There sitting on a branch high up in the branches was a grey squirrel staring at them.

"Why do you think it's staring at us?" asked Matthew.

"I have no idea, but it is definitely staring right at us," Leo replied. "I wonder what it's thinking?"

The squirrel sat perfectly still, but suddenly cocked his head to one side, twitched his whiskers and shook his tail. He was off before the boys could say anything and it bounded across the branches and out of sight. Leo and Matthew looked at each other, shrugged their shoulders and continued their hunt.

They had not gone very far when Leo suddenly became aware of a familiar sound in the distance. It didn't seem to fit with the normal noises of the forest and the feeling of uneasiness started to return. He gestured to

Matthew to stop and put his finger up to his lips. Matthew stood still and they both listened carefully. Leo was sure that he had heard a ticking sound. It reminded him of staring at the classroom clock. Matthew was about to say something when Leo grabbed his arm. "Shhh!" he whispered. "There it is again; I think I can hear something."

The boys stood totally still and listened again, but there were no ticking noises. A pinecone fell from a tree, bouncing off the branches. Perhaps Leo had heard that. A bird tweeted in the tree above and there was the gentle rustling of leaves, but there was nothing out of the ordinary.

"I can't hear anything," whispered Matthew, "I think you imagined it. Come on let's keep looking."

They relaxed and started walking forward when suddenly they both stopped dead. "Tick, tick, tick," there was no mistaking it now, they could both hear the ticking noise.

"I can hear it too!" said Matthew, "What is it?"

"It's coming from over there," said Leo, "Behind that bush."

"Maybe the squirrel has laid a trap for us!" giggled Matthew.

Leo snorted at the thought, and the two boys crept forward, a little worried about what they might find on the other side of the undergrowth. As they got closer the ticking sound got louder. Leo got down on his hands and knees and peered through the branches of a large fern.

"Matthew, look!" exclaimed Leo, "There's a big mushroom on the other side of the bush."

"That's not a mushroom, it's too big," said Matthew as he knelt next to Leo, "That's a toadstool, I think, although it's very big and an odd colour for a toadstool. It sounds like the ticking is coming from behind it!"

They pushed their way through the thick ferns and came out into a mossy clearing on the other side. The toadstool was the only one they could see, and it stood in the middle of the clearing. It was an odd-looking toadstool. Not red and spotty like the ones Leo and Matthew had seen in cartoons and fairy tales. This toadstool was very big, had a large smooth top that was golden in colour and this was attached to quite a fat black stem.

43

As the boys walked around the large, peculiar toadstool, they realised that the ticking was not coming from behind it… the ticking was coming from inside it! The ticking was also getting quicker, which began to panic them a little. Leo stepped closer and put his ear against the soft golden top of the toadstool. He lifted his head in surprise and then put it down again.

"I can hear something!" he said to Matthew.

"What is it?" Matthew replied anxiously.

Leo pressed his ear against the toadstool once more. "I think… I think it's a voice!"

"Help! Help! Let me out!" came a muffled cry from inside the toadstool.

Leo jumped back in surprise. "Quick, I think there's someone stuck inside the toadstool!"

"A person?" shouted Matthew. "But how would they get inside?"

"I don't know! But he's shouting for help!" yelled Leo. They hurriedly started to pull at the golden top of the toadstool, but it would not budge. The ticking was getting quicker and quicker. They pulled again with all their might, but it just would not move.

"Maybe there's a hidden lever, or a button, or something," Matthew shouted hurriedly, and they started to run their hands all over the toadstool. Suddenly, Leo felt a slightly spongy area at the base of the black stem that was different from the rest of the toadstool. He followed his instinct and gave it a hard push. Instantly, there was a loud POP as the top of the toadstool flipped back off the stem. This was followed by a loud BANG! The boys fell backwards under a shower of green sparks. They both covered their faces, but Leo saw something shoot out of the toadstool, high into the air and land with an almighty thud at their feet. The lid of the toadstool flipped shut and the ticking stopped. Leo and Matthew held their breath, not daring to move. There was only one thought on their minds, 'What had come out of the toadstool?'

4

Trapped

The two boys stared at the strange heap lying on the ground in front of them. What was it? Was it alive? Was it dead? Leo glanced around and thought he saw a flash of orange in the ferns, on the other side of the clearing. He wanted to look more closely but he could not move. The heap in front of them was a muddy green and grey colour and lay as still as a rock. Without any warning, it twitched, and then let out a groan. Leo and Matthew stood up very quickly and backed away from whatever it was. They glanced at each other, unsure of what to do next.

Leo slowly turned around and snapped a twig from a bush. He glanced at Matthew nervously before stepping forwards and giving the strange heap a sharp poke with his stick. The heap let out a loud "Owwweeeeeeeeee!" and a small man leapt up and ran straight at the boys. Leo and Matthew screamed and had just enough time to dive onto the ground as the man flew right between them and crashed into the spiky undergrowth behind them.

"Owwweeeeeeeeee!" he screeched for a second time and the man started hopping madly around the clearing, pulling thorns out from his side.

Leo and Matthew could only sit and stare in disbelief at such a strange sight. The small jumping man finally slowed down and came to a stop. He turned around slowly so they could see his unusually round face. He looked like a man, but a very small man. There was something else too, something strange about him; he had small, pointed ears. He stared straight at Leo and Matthew and his lips snarled defensively at the corner of his mouth. He had large piercing green eyes, which did not blink, and he just kept staring.

Leo and Matthew didn't know what to do other than stare straight back. They were mesmerised. The man was small and stocky, he looked strong. He could be no taller than Leo and Matthew's waist. He had long flowing silver-white hair, a long white beard and those bright green eyes. He was wearing a tall, pointed bottle-green hat, muddy grey clothes and he had thick black boots on. There was a large shiny emerald-green ring on one of his fingers. He looked a little bit like the pictures of gnomes or elves that the boys had seen in books.

"Who are you?" he whispered urgently in a deep voice. He kept on staring at them but also seemed very anxious. "Who sent you? How did you open the..." he paused glancing around, "the locking toadstool?" he hissed.

Leo turned and looked at Matthew, who looked like he was in as much shock as he was, with his mouth wide open. Who was this small man? Was he dangerous? Leo decided that he needed to say something quickly.

"My name is Leo, and this is Matthew," he said in a shaky voice. "We were exploring the forest and we heard the ticking inside that toadstool. We came to have a look and we heard you shouting for help. We were trying to set you free. We thought we were helping!"

The mysterious man relaxed a little. He glanced around nervously and said in a hurried voice, "It's not safe here. There are spies in the forest. We need to get away. Come with me, quickly!"

Before Leo and Matthew had a chance to say anything the small man pulled them towards the far side of the clearing and back into the forest again. They ran through the ferns quickly until they stopped by an old oak tree. The small man reached up and put his finger, the one with the shiny emerald ring on it, into a tiny hole in the tree. There was a click, like the sound of a lock undoing, and from somewhere above, a thick vine dropped out of the oak tree and dangled above them.

"Hurry! Grab hold, like me," said the man.

Leo and Matthew really didn't have time to think about it and they grabbed hold of the vine. Immediately, the vine wrapped itself around their arms, yanked them off their feet and pulled them up into the air, towards the top of the tree. Leo tried to look up as they swung up through the branches, bumping into boughs on the way. He could see that they were heading towards a large nest that sat on a thick branch, high up in the tree. Leo felt sick with fear and was terrified about what they might find in the nest, but he knew the vine would not let go of him now.

The vine pulled all three of them over the side of the nest and out of view from the forest floor. To their horror, Leo and Matthew then noticed that there was no bottom to the nest and instead there was just an empty dark hole in the branch. The small man let go of the vine, rolled down the side of the nest and dropped into the hole.

The boys did not even have a choice, the vine slipped from their fingers and they tumbled down the mossy sides of the nest and, before they could stop themselves, they plunged into the empty dark hole.

They had not fallen far when they landed with a bump on a shiny, slippery surface. Without knowing where it would take them, they slid down the smooth tunnel inside the thick branch. It was only a short slide until they were spat out into a dark circular area that had been hollowed out from the centre of the tree. They tumbled into the centre of the room.

Leo and Matthew sat up and dusted themselves down, as their eyes slowly adjusted to the darkness. They peered around and realised that there was nothing much in the dark space except them and the strange little man. The man was squatting down at the back of the space and was staring at them again. His green eyes glowed in the darkness.

"Where are we? What's happening to us?" whispered Matthew anxiously.

Leo didn't know what to say. He looked at the man and decided to try and find out; "Who are you? Why have you brought us here?" Leo was not sure if he and Matthew were in danger or not. The man kept on staring, his bright green eyes never blinking.

"Where are we?" Matthew asked. Leo could tell that Matthew was scared too.

Leo looked round the space trying to find a way out, but the small man slowly stood up. Leo locked his eyes back on the strange man, and his inquisitive green eyes never left the two boys. He finally spoke in a deep smooth voice, "You are in a Holding Nest."

"A Holding Nest?" said Matthew. "What's a Holding Nest? Does that mean we are prisoners?"

The man smiled and said quietly, "Not yet Mr. Matthew, but you never know in this forest. Holding Nests are used by our kind, to escape from the dangers of the forest. They can only be opened with a ring like mine," and he held up the ring on his finger. "We are safe here."

Leo and Matthew thought this sounded very odd but didn't want to say anything that might upset their captor.

The piercing green eyes began to relax a little and the little man seemed happy that Leo and Matthew were not going to harm him. He seemed to hesitate though, unsure of what to do next. Eventually, he took a step towards the two boys, who shrank back in fear. The man smiled and holding out his hand, he said, "I am very sorry if I have scared you, I mean you no harm. Let me introduce myself. My name is Sorrel. I am a forest gnelf."

5

Forest Gnelves

Leo and Matthew stared at Sorrel. The snarling lips had softened into a broad smile and the boys could see his gleaming teeth. The emerald eyes were still piercing, but much warmer now. They gingerly shook his hand, not really sure if they trusted him.

"A forest what?" said Leo, "A gnelf? I've never heard of a gnelf before," he paused before continuing, "What is a gnelf? Is it like an elf? I've heard of gnomes and elves and other magical people. Are you... are you one of them?"

Sorrel sighed and raised his eyebrows slightly, "We are nothing like them. Gnomes and elves are what human people, like you, have believed in for many years.

You have no idea about the truth. Gnelves have existed since the beginning of time. We live all around you, but you never see us. We try very hard never to interact with humankind."

Matthew, who had been sitting very still, said quietly, "So, where do you live and why were you trapped inside that toadstool?" He was being much more cautious than Leo.

"Listen," Sorrel began, "I will explain in due course, but I have frightened you and I'm very sorry. You must be thirsty." He scuttled over to a small hatch in the wood, which a tiny cupboard lay behind. Sorrel pulled out a bottle and held it out to the boys. "Here, drink this, it's only water. Nothing magic, I promise."

Leo reached out and took the bottle. "What are you doing?" whispered Matthew, "You have no idea what it is!"

"Mr. Matthew is right," agreed Sorrel. He took the bottle back from Leo, opened it and took a swig himself. Nothing happened. "See!" he said smiling, "It's just water. Please trust me."

Leo took the bottle again, looked at Matthew, who clearly disapproved, and he said, "Why would he want to harm us? We saved him from the toadstool." Leo put the bottle up to his lips and took a gulp. To his relief, he realised it was only water. The cool water was very refreshing, and after a long drink he passed it to Matthew. "Go on, I promise, it's fine!"

Matthew hesitated before taking a sip. He waited to see if anything would happen and then took a longer drink. Meanwhile, Sorrel had pulled out a small bag from the cupboard and gestured for them to help themselves. Leo gladly selected one of the bright green sweets. He popped it in his mouth and gave it a suck. He smiled when he realised it tasted like a mint butterscotch. "Yum!" he exclaimed. This was one step too far for Matthew, who politely declined the sweet.

"Dewdrops are my favourite," said Sorrel popping another one in his mouth, "Every Holding Nest has some, so if we ever have to take refuge in one, we will always find water and something to eat."

Matthew, who had begun to relax a little, wanted to know more about who Sorrel was.

"Of course, let me explain," began Sorrel, "My people, the forest gnelves, are wonderful, kind people. We are peaceful and we mind our own business, but not all gnelves are like us. There is one gnelf, who is not like us. She is wicked and mean. Her name is Devellza. She is a dark gnelf and she has become our most feared enemy." Sorrel paused to see whether it was too much information for them, but they gestured for him to continue. "She is the leader of the dark gnelves and their workers too; the quokkerwodgers. Devellza wants to be the most powerful gnelf in the land. She is building up an army of dark gnelves and quokkerwodgers. They have stolen something very precious that belongs to the forest gnelves. She has taken the Conifer Crown from our gnelfdom, where we live. The Conifer Crown is vital for our way of life. So, our Conifer, the leader of the forest gnelves, sent some of us out to see if we could find the Conifer Crown and return it to our gnelfdom."

The boys stared wide-eyed at Sorrel. He continued, "We were following some dark gnelves through the shadows of this forest, but a squirrel spy spotted us and told the dark gnelves where we were."

Leo and Matthew glanced at each other with the mention of a squirrel spy. Maybe the grey squirrel they had seen at the edge of the forest was more dangerous than they had realised.

Sorrel continued, "The dark gnelves attacked us and we were all split up. Unfortunately, they caught me, and it was them that imprisoned me in the locking toadstool. I was desperate to get out. Locking toadstools are very powerful and once someone is shut inside, they can only be released before the next sunset, or else they turn into a dark gnelf."

"Wow!" said Leo, who had been listening very carefully. "Lucky we found you when we did. That sounds awful, but I have so many questions. What exactly is the Conifer Crown? Why is it so important?"

Sorrel hesitated. Had he already told the boys too much? He knew the forest gnelves needed help and perhaps these boys were the answer. He had already shown them a Holding Nest. He decided to take the risk.

"The Conifer Crown belongs to the forest gnelves. It is our life-source. It provides the energy for our gnelfdom and gives the forest gnelves their magic powers. You see, each gnelfdom has its own life source. For example, the sand gnelves have a Conch Crown and we, the forest gnelves, have a Conifer Crown. The Conifer Crown never dies, it lives forever and gives us our powers. It keeps us safe, but now it has been taken, stolen by Devellza. The forest gnelves are getting weaker and we are losing our powers. Soon, we will not be able to protect our homes from Devellza and the army of dark gnelves. She wants to take over our gnelfdom and rule over all the forest gnelves. She won't stop until she controls all the gnelfdoms."

Leo and Matthew could not believe what they were hearing. Forest gnelves, dark gnelves and other gnelfdoms, it was all new to them and a lot to take in. Here was Sorrel, a forest gnelf, who was trying to find the Conifer Crown, that had been stolen by Devellza. He was alone and the dark gnelves had imprisoned him in a locking toadstool hoping he would become one of them. Now he was with them in a Holding Nest. The boys felt sorry for Sorrel and Leo knew that he wanted to help him, if they could.

"Let us come with you, Sorrel. We will help the forest gnelves find the Conifer Crown and return it to your gnelfdom," Leo said in a determined way. He was surprised at how brave he sounded.

Matthew was about to argue with Leo but saw the determination on his face. He looked at Sorrel and his gut told him that they would be doing the right thing. He sighed.

"Yes," agreed Matthew, "Please let us come too. We can help you with your fight against Devellza and the dark gnelves. They sound horrible."

Sorrel seemed deep in thought, weighing up the options, and stared at the two boys with his large green eyes. Eventually, he said, "Thank you for your offer Mr. Leo and Mr. Matthew, you are very kind, both of you, but I cannot accept your offer. It is too dangerous, and it is already too much that you have seen me. Very few humans have ever met a gnelf. Taking you with me will expose you to things in our world that you should never know about. You must forget about me and go back to your lives as normal."

"Listen Sorrel," said Leo, "We might not have any magic powers, or know anything about the gnelf world, but we can learn. We are bigger and stronger than you, or any other gnelf. We can help protect you. Besides, you have already been caught once, so perhaps you do need our help after all."

This was true, and Sorrel knew Leo was right. He hesitated before agreeing, "Okay Mr. Leo, I will let you help me, but you do not know Devellza. She is a very dark gnelf and she will hurt you if she can."

"She doesn't scare us, and you can use your powers to protect us," said Matthew, surprised at his own change of heart.

"Yes, right, that's settled then," said Leo, trying to sound convincing and secretly pleased that Matthew was supporting him. He didn't want to think about a dark gnelf who was out to hurt him. "Besides, you have others that can help too, don't you?"

"No, Mr. Leo, it would only be us. The other forest gnelves will be needed to protect our gnelfdom," sighed Sorrel.

"Well, I'm sure we'll be okay without them, don't you agree Matthew? What do we need to do first, Sorrel?"

Matthew didn't have a chance to reply before Sorrel continued, "First, I must return home," replied Sorrel. "I need to consult with the Conifer and the members of her council. If you are to come with me, I must gather a few things for our journey. I will let you back down to the forest floor and we will meet back at the oak tree in a few hours, just after sunset. But remember, if you see a squirrel, then act normally and they will ignore you. They are very used to seeing humans, but they are all spies for the dark gnelves, and we do not want them becoming suspicious."

So, the vines lowered the boys and Sorrel back down through the leafy boughs to the ground again. Cautiously, Sorrel showed Leo and Matthew through the undergrowth and back to the beach.

Before he left, Sorrel made a solemn promise to them that he would return later and meet them after sunset. He also made them promise not to say a word to anyone about what they had seen or heard. However, Sorrel didn't need to worry as both Leo and Matthew would never dare spoil what had already been such a wonderfully strange and eventful day. They didn't want it to stop and they both swore that they would not tell Leo's parents or the girls anything about what they had seen or heard.

They left Sorrel and started to run back along the beach. Leo glanced over his shoulder at the forest and saw another flicker of orange in the brambles. Again, Leo squinted at it, trying to see what it was, but it vanished. Perhaps it was the setting sun.

67

Before they reached the campsite, Matthew grabbed Leo's arm and stopped him from going through the rickety gate. "Leo, wait, do you think we can trust Sorrel? We don't know anything about him. What if he's lying? Maybe he's the evil one! We could get ourselves into big trouble."

Leo puzzled over this for a moment and then said "Yes, maybe he is lying, but Matthew, why would he tell us all that information, and then let us go? He could have poisoned us with the dewdrops, but he didn't. He could have left us in the Holding Nest, but he didn't. I think I believe what he said, and anyway, we are much bigger than he is. Plus, I really think he needs our help. His whole gnelfdom does. We could actually make a difference, and this could be a real adventure!"

"But…. he's a gnelf!! I mean, what is that? Are we even awake?" Matthew exclaimed.

"Yes, it's definitely real," replied Leo. "All I know is that he needs us, whatever he is. And it is quite exciting too!" he exclaimed. "Look, why don't we take Rocket with us. She can stay by our side and she will protect us. Besides, she's the size of a horse for a gnelf!"

The boys giggled and agreed to take Rocket. If they felt unsafe then they would run away from Sorrel and come straight back to the campsite.

However, as Leo and Matthew walked up to the campsite, they both secretly knew that this might end up being a much bigger adventure than either of them had ever bargained for.

6

No Turning Back

*B*ack at the campsite, Leo and Matthew found it very difficult to sit still for dinner. Mr. Dickens was barbequing sausages and Mrs. Dickens was making a salad. Issy and Rosie demanded an extra chair was set at the table, for their chosen teddy to join them for dinner. Everything seemed to take so long. Leo and Matthew had cleverly hatched a plan to tell Leo's parents that they had built a den and wanted to camp out in the forest overnight. The boys didn't know how long they would be with Sorrel, but the last thing they needed was Leo's mother or father coming to look for them. Leo's father had scoffed at the idea and said they would probably come home halfway through the night; cold and miserable. Eventually, Leo's parents had both agreed to let the boys try, as long as they had Rocket with them and a mobile phone in case of emergencies.

Finally, dinner was over, and the restless boys quickly packed their pockets with anything they thought might be useful, and said they were going back to their den before the sun set.

"I've got a torch, some matches, a few biscuits, Mum's phone and Dad's penknife," said Leo in a hushed voice. "Is that enough? I've got Rocket's lead too. Do we need anything else?"

"I don't know!" said Matthew, "I've never helped a forest gnelf before!"

"Shhh! Don't let them hear you," hissed Leo glancing round at his family. Thankfully Issy was not eavesdropping for once. "Right Mum, we're off!" shouted Leo as he and Matthew headed out of the campsite.

"Okay, but make sure you do not go into the sea please and make sure you come back if it starts raining!" shouted Leo's mother as the two boys hurtled off towards the rickety gate out of the campsite, with Rocket running besides them. Leo yelled back, promising that they would, but he knew very well that his parents would soon be too busy playing Rummy with their campervan neighbours to worry too much about them. Annoyingly, Mrs. Dickens had made them take a bag with their sleeping bags in it, which of course they knew they would not need, but they could not argue that, so they then had to hide the bag under a bush on the way to the beach, so it would not get in the way.

Leo and Matthew ran down the mossy path and back along the beach to the edge of the forest. The sun was just setting on the horizon as they ventured into the forest to find the oak tree. Leo put Rocket on her lead, so they didn't lose her. They were wearing their walking boots and Leo was glad he had brought the torch. They had no idea where Sorrel was going to take them.

They passed the clearing with the locking toadstool, which thankfully was not ticking this time, and soon they came upon the large oak tree that disappeared into the leafy canopy above. The boys stopped by the base of the trunk and sat on a large root poking out from the ground. They waited and they waited, keeping an eye out for any squirrels. They waited for what seemed an eternity until Matthew whispered to Leo, "It's getting really dark.

What happens if Sorrel doesn't come? What will we do?"

Leo was thinking of a reply when a soft rustling noise caught his attention. He looked over towards a rock lying next to some ferns, but nothing moved. Everything seemed still and quiet again. He squinted in the darkness and then he noticed the rock began to move. He grabbed Matthew's arm and pointed at the rock. The boys shrank back in terror. The rock grew slowly and started to transform into the shape of a man. Then, they realised, to their relief, that it was only Sorrel.

"Sorrel, you scared us. Have you been there the whole time?" Leo asked.

"Yes, I wanted to make sure you hadn't been followed," Sorrel replied. Leo and Matthew glanced nervously around them. As they stood up, Rocket stood up too and padded over to Sorrel, who reached up and gave her a rub under her chin. The boys stared in surprise.

"But are you not scared of Rocket? She's twice your size," asked Leo curiously.

"Mr. Leo, if we feared every dog, we would never be able to cross human gardens. We just smell like rocks to dogs, so they only chase us if we run."

"Well, I thought you were a rock! That's amazing camouflage," Matthew said.

Sorrel grinned, "We have been hiding as rocks for hundreds of years. Our magic can make our clothes so stiff and cold that we look and feel like rocks. You never know, you may have sat on a gnelf before and just never realised it."

Leo and Matthew looked at each other horrified, and Leo suddenly remembered the two rocks he had seen from the car, that he had mistaken for rabbits. Maybe they had not been rocks or rabbits, but before he could say anything, Sorrel continued, "Are you ready to help the forest gnelves, and help me find the Conifer Crown? We need to get it back to our people as soon as possible, so the Conifer has reluctantly given you her blessing to help. Initially, she was not happy I had revealed my true identity to you, so I had to persuade her, but it's not too late for you to say no."

The boys quickly said they both wanted to do anything they could to help. Sorrel beckoned them a little closer and whispered in a hushed voice, "Beware of the shadows. The dark gnelves and the quokkerwodgers move in the shadows. They often roam freely and they creep around in the darkness. You will always know a dark gnelf because they wear black pointed hats, wear black rings on their fingers and their eyes are as black as the shadows that they live in."

Leo and Matthew peered around nervously, suddenly very uneasy, and it seemed like all the shadows in the forest now looked dark and menacing, with hidden secrets.

Sorrel saw the expressions on their faces and he quickly added, "Listen, I will know if a dark gnelf is nearby. My sensor-ring will vibrate against my finger Every gnelf has one and it acts as a warning when a dark gnelf is nearby."

"So, how did they catch you and put you in a locking toadstool?" asked Leo.

"Remember Mr. Leo, I was following them. I knew the dark gnelves were nearby, but my sensor-ring doesn't warn me against the squirrel spies," replied Sorrel. "Now, we should go. We shouldn't stay in one place for too long. Follow me and try not to make a sound."

Leo and Matthew hardly had time to look at each other before they were forced to follow Sorrel through the undergrowth. Another flash of orange in the undergrowth caught Leo's eye, but try as he might, it was too dark to see where it had come from and Rocket didn't seem to notice anything, so maybe he had been mistaken.

Leo and Matthew were not sure where they were going, or what they were going to have to do. Where was Sorrel taking them? Would it be scary or perhaps it would be dangerous? Maybe they really could help Sorrel and save the forest gnelves from the evil clutches of Devellza, or maybe not, but one thing was for certain, Leo and Matthew realised that this was going to be a night unlike any other they had experienced before.

7

The Warrinth

Sorrel led Leo and Matthew quickly and quietly through the trees, jumping over twisted roots and darting through the undergrowth. The air was still, and the forest was silent, except the occasional cry of a seagull and the rustle of the leaves in the evening breeze. Occasionally, Sorrel would stop and stand perfectly still, listening to the sounds of the forest before setting off again. At one point, Sorrel did a nimble little cartwheel over some roots and Leo stopped dead in astonishment.

"I knew it!" he said to himself, realising that the cartwheeling rabbit he had seen at school might have been a gnelf.

"Come on, Leo! We've got to keep up!" pleaded Matthew.

Sorrel moved nimbly and silently over the roots and through the brambles and ferns. Rocket did too, but the two boys were less nimble and found it quite difficult to keep up. More than once they tripped over a stubborn root. Leo and Matthew were concentrating so hard on where they were going, as well as not making a noise, that at one point they suddenly realised that Sorrel was no longer in front of them. He had vanished! They glanced wildly around them, desperately seeking a glimpse of his grey clothing or green hat. They didn't want to use their torch but maybe they would have to. Then suddenly they caught sight of Sorrel's green pointed hat. He was standing at the base of a large tree with a tall thick trunk.

"I'm so sorry," he whispered as they caught up to him, "I was thinking about Devellza and her army of dark gnelves. I completely forgot that you hadn't used the warrinth before, but don't worry, it's very easy!"

"The what!? The warrinth? What is the warrinth?" hissed Matthew, concerned. "Is it dangerous?"

"No, no, don't worry, it's not at all dangerous," replied Sorrel. "The warrinth is our network of underground shafts and tunnels that the gnelves use to travel from one place to another. The warrinth uses magic and natural powers from the orb of the compass-clock, which is at the heart of the warrinth, to carry gnelves from one place to another. You'll see what I mean. You always access the warrinth through a tree. Look up there!" and Sorrel pointed to a hole, high up in the trunk. "That is where the guard of the warrinth sits. Each entrance to the warrinth has one and the guards are always owls. We call them sowldiers."

Leo giggled but quickly stopped when he saw Sorrel's serious face.

"It's no laughing matter Mr. Leo. The sowldiers do us a great service and we must show them the utmost respect. Any tree that has a hole and a sowldier, is an entry point to the warrinth." Leo and Matthew looked up at the hole and saw two large round owl eyes appear in the darkness. "But we can't take Rocket with us. We must leave her here, tied to the tree. Don't worry, she will be perfectly safe. The sowldier will keep an eye on her."

The boys reluctantly agreed, and Leo tied Rocket's lead around a branch, patting her head lovingly. "Don't worry Rocket, we'll be back soon," he said, and Rocket whined softly, knowing she was being left behind.

"But how do we get into the warrinth and won't we get lost?" said Matthew in a worried voice.

"Ah, getting in to the warrinth is very easy. I can show you, but you need one of these." Sorrel pulled out two green gnelf hats from his inside pocket and passed one each to Leo and Matthew. "They adapt their size to fit your head. Put them on and then when you get inside, you need to tell the warrinth where you want to go. Wait for the Secretan to ask you."

"Who is the Secretan?" asked Leo worriedly.

"The Secretan guards the compass-clock and controls the movements of all the gnelves through the warrinth. The Secretan is extremely powerful. You will not see him; you will only hear his voice."

"But where are we going?" interrupted Matthew.

"We are going to the Kolldor Caves. Remember that name. Shout it out when the Secretan asks where you are going. That is one of the places where we can find the dark gnelves and it is where the forest gnelf elders think that the dark gnelves have taken the Conifer Crown. Now, do exactly as I do, don't stop, just keep running!"

Before Leo or Matthew could stop him, Sorrel turned around and ran full pelt towards the tree. He didn't stop. He ran straight into the tree, and with a sudden hoot from the sowldier, he was gone. He had not gone around it or bounced off it, he had disappeared straight into the middle of it, but he had not come out the other side either.

"What? No way! Where's he gone? We can't do that! We're not magic!" Matthew exclaimed. "Maybe this is when we should go home Leo. I'm scared now, we can't do this, let's go back to the campsite." Rocket whimpered in sympathy.

Leo closed his eyes and tried to push his own worries aside. He desperately wanted to agree with Matthew, but he knew he needed to be confident. In the classroom, Mrs. Shackleton always talked about confidence, resilience and perseverance. They were the school values, and this was one of those moments. Sorrel needed their help, so there was no way they could leave now. Leo opened his eyes and turned to Matthew, "Matthew, I feel the same, but we can't leave, Sorrel needs us. That's why we have these gnelf hats, to keep us safe." Leo held up his hat. "We have to try! We have to follow him."

Leo looked straight at the tree. This was what he had wanted – a real adventure and he was not going to give up now. He had to be brave. Before Matthew could stop him, Leo pulled the hat onto his head. He could feel a tingling magic as the hat quickly adjusted its size, until it fit snugly, and then he was off. Leo ran straight at the tree and as he got closer, he braced himself for the painful impact. He was not magic; he knew he was about to head-butt the tree… but it never happened. The last thing Leo heard was the distinct hoot of the tree sowldier as he disappeared into the tree and down into the deep dark tunnels of the warrinth.

Leo was flying! The air whistled past him. He slowly opened his eyes and looked around him. He was no longer in the forest. Instead, he was hurtling down a long dark tunnel. There were lanterns along the walls that glowed with a green light and green moss covered the ground and the walls. He panicked and started to thrash about. He kept thinking he was about to fly into the side, as he somersaulted through the air, tumbling along.

However, he realised that he was never actually touching the walls, and he was always being pulled back into the centre of the tunnel. As he flew downwards a strange soothing voice came from nowhere, "The warrinth welcomes you. Where are you travelling to?" Leo looked all around. Who was that? He realised he was no longer spinning around, and he began to relax, flying more steadily. He could not tell where the voice was coming from, but it seemed to be all around him. He thought back to what Sorrel had said about the Secretan and the instructions. He took a deep breath and shouted, "The Kolldor Caves!"

8

The Kolldor Caves

Leo could not do anything except let his body be taken by the vacuum that pulled him through the tunnels of the warrinth. He continued to wobble a bit and fly from side to side a little, but quickly he began to get the hang of it, and he glided more steadily as his confidence grew. Now, Leo could look around him a little bit more and he could not believe he was flying! Or was he gliding? Maybe he was falling? He was not really sure, but whatever it was, he smiled as now he knew what it was like to fly like a superhero or to be weightless like an astronaut. It was a wonderful feeling. Leo noticed that there were lots of junctions with other tunnels and that some tunnels were wider than others. He also realised that there were other gnelves too, that looked just like Sorrel, all travelling through the warrinth, flying the same way that he was. They zipped from tunnel to tunnel, this way and that. Most of the time he only got a glimpse of their grey rock-like coats and a flash of colour from their hats before they disappeared down other tunnels. Some even read newspapers as they whizzed along. They didn't seem to notice or care that an imposter was using their warrinth. He noticed that different gnelves had different coloured hats and he wondered what that meant.

Soon, Leo's tunnel opened into a large chamber and he flew in. Gnelves were again zipping past him, in all directions. At the bottom of the chamber was a large wheel with twelve pointed arrows on it, which reminded Leo of a large compass. That must be the compass-clock he thought, and he wondered where the Secretan was. In the centre of the compass was an orb of golden light. Leo didn't have time to notice anything else before he had crossed the chamber and started to fly down a different tunnel. However, this tunnel was different from the last. No longer was there any green moss, but now a layer of dead leaves carpeted the tunnel, the walls were covered in a chocolate-coloured mud and the lanterns gave out a hazel-coloured glow.

Before long, Leo veered down a tunnel to the right and then ominously the tunnels started becoming a little colder and less well-lit. Suddenly, before he knew what was happening, Leo shot out of a tree and he was back on his feet running across the ground, away from the tree trunk. The shock of being on his own two feet was too much for him and Leo promptly tripped and tumbled forward onto the ground. He landed with a thud at Sorrel's feet. Leo was just picking himself up when there was a hoot from a sowldier behind him, and Matthew suddenly appeared from inside the tree. Leo watched as Matthew managed to slow his run and bring himself to stop without falling over.

"Well done, Mr. Matthew," said Sorrel impressed. "Never you mind Mr. Leo, first timers normally do fall over," and he helped Leo get back on his feet.

"Wow! What just happened? That was amazing," gushed Matthew, who was still trying to take everything in. "We were flying! That was so cool. Was that the compass-clock we saw? Where did all those tunnels lead to?"

Sorrel decided it was safe enough to explain a little more to the boys, "Come closer both of you. Yes, that was the compass-clock we passed, and all those tunnels lead to different gnelfdoms. The other gnelves you saw were moving between gnelfdoms. That golden ball of light at the centre of the compass-clock is what feeds the energy out to our life-sources like the Conifer Crown. The compass-clock takes its energy from the centre of the Earth and it is what the Secretan protects."

"I had no idea anything like that existed!" said Leo amazed. "So, where are we now?"

Sorrel glanced around before continuing, "This area is an old, abandoned part of our land that not many gnelves have ever been to. Not long ago, our cousins, the cave gnelves, lived here and the caves were bright and beautiful, with crystals in the walls that danced in the firelight and glistening stalactites hung from the ceilings. Those were peaceful times. Dark gnelves existed then but they lived in small groups scattered around the land. Dark gnelves had no leader and no power. That was until Devellza arrived and decided she wanted power. She wanted the caves for herself and for the dark gnelves to live in. You see, Devellza did not have a fixed home either and she had no life-source to rely on. So, she gathered the dark gnelves together and she organised an attack on the Kolldor Caves. The cave gnelves were taken by surprise and Devellza quickly took control of the caves, forcing our cousins to flee. The cave gnelves had no choice but to abandon their life-source; the Crystal Crown, and they fled to new homes elsewhere. They now rely on the life-sources of others, but one day they will need to return. The Kolldor Caves became the home for the dark gnelves and Devellza was made their leader. However, the dark gnelves are mean and lazy and Devellza quickly made slaves out of the peaceful quokkerwodgers, who now serve the dark gnelves. Ever since, this place has become dark and powerless and the Crystal Crown's power has lessened in the wrong hands. Devellza is planning to steal the life-sources from the other gnelfdoms because she can use them here. If she brings all the life-sources together, then they will feed off one another and this will become the most powerful gnelfdom of all. Only then would she be able to challenge the Secretan, control our magic and rule over all of us."

"The poor cave gnelves, how horrid and unfair for them, and now she has your life-source too! We need to stop her. So, is Devellza here now?" asked Matthew in a worried voice.

"No," replied Sorrel pointing into the distance. "She lives in the grandest cave of them all, at the top of the cliff, over that ridge. That's where she keeps the Crystal Crown too."

"Okay, so what do we need to do now?" asked Leo.

"Our wise leader, the Conifer, believes that the Conifer Crown has been brought to the Kolldor Caves by the dark gnelves," Sorrel continued. "They are keeping it here before they deliver it to Devellza. We need to try to get the Conifer Crown before it reaches Devellza. Look at the sky, there is a full moon today, a special day for the dark gnelves, so our forest elders think it would make sense that the Conifer Crown is presented to Devellza tonight."

"Don't you think you should come back here with backup, with more of the forest gnelves?" whispered Matthew.

"No, Mr. Matthew," Sorrel reminded him. "All of our kind are needed to protect our gnelfdom. We don't know how many dark gnelves there are out in the forest. Besides, I told the Conifer that I had two human warriors to help me."

"Warriors? We're not warriors!" hissed Matthew. "We're just two friends from Silverdale!"

"Shush!" Leo hissed back. "We are brave!" He turned back to Sorrel, "We can be warriors if we need to be. So, what's the plan?"

Sorrel ignored Matthew's concerns and concentrated on the matter in hand. "Right, well, we have the element of surprise on our side and they definitely won't be expecting humans either. We'll ambush them as they leave the cave, grab the Conifer Crown and then get back to the warrinth as quickly as possible."

Sorrel turned and moved away before they could ask any more questions. Leo and Matthew followed him quickly and quietly as they slipped between the shadows and tip-toed their way along the base of the mountainside cliffs to the entrance of the caves. They kept looking around anxiously, in case any dark gnelf or quokkerwodger on guard might spot them. They had not gone far when Sorrel stopped dead in his tracks and spun around. He frantically dragged the boys under some ferns and signalled to them not to make a sound. Leo and Matthew lay completely still, terrified of making a noise. Sorrel pointed upwards and as Leo and Matthew looked up a movement in the branches of a nearby tree caught their attention. Out onto a branch jumped a grey squirrel. A squirrel spy! The squirrel stopped and looked around cautiously, his nose twitching. He cocked his head and listened carefully until he seemed satisfied and bounded off between the branches.

"Phew! That was close!" whispered Sorrel. "We need to move on, in case he comes back. There might be others."

9

Dark Gnelves

*T*he trio carefully crawled out of the ferns and continued on their way. The reality of what they were doing began to sink in, but Leo only had to think about the poor cave gnelves, who had lost their home, and he knew he had to keep going. He didn't want Sorrel and the other forest gnelves losing their homes too. However, the closer Leo and Matthew got to the mouth of the Kolldor Caves the more nervous they began to feel.

As they crept forward, Leo wished he had paid more attention in those history lessons. He desperately tried to remember the Roman fighting techniques that Mrs. Shackleton had been teaching them about, but it was no use. Matthew had a furrowed expression on his face and looked like he was trying to remember the same thing. Leo suddenly felt a pang of guilt. Had he led his best friend into danger? Matthew had not been sure from the beginning; he had not even eaten one of those dewdrops in the Holding Nest. Maybe he should have listened to Matthew back then. Should he have thought more carefully about what he was doing, like his mother always said he should? Probably. On the other hand, he could not believe how brave he was being. He rather liked the new, more confident Leo. He was proud of Matthew too. He didn't have time to finish his train of thought as Sorrel stopped and beckoned them to crouch behind a large rock.

"That's the entrance, over there," said Sorrel pointing ahead to a large opening in the mountainside. "That's the entrance they will use. We need to position ourselves on either side of it. You two stay on this side, I'll go to the other and when I whistle, you must both charge out and attack whoever is in front of you. There will be dark gnelves and quokkerwodgers. None of them have ever been seen by humans before, they will be terrified. So, whilst you distract them, I'll slip past and grab the

Conifer Crown. Then, we must all run to that large tree over there." Sorrel pointed across the rocky ground to a large fir tree standing proudly on its own on the edge of the forest. "It's the nearest entry point into the warrinth. Make sure you do not lose your hats!"

Leo and Matthew both instinctively pulled their green gnelf hats down tighter around their ears.

"Good!" smiled Sorrel. "Now grab a large stick as a weapon and follow me."

They grabbed a heavy stick each and Sorrel led Leo and Matthew along the steep walls of the cliff. The three of them squeezed into a crack in the wall just to the side of the entrance.

"Wait here," whispered Sorrel, "and remember, go on my whistle." As Sorrel turned to go, he paused and turned back to the boys, "the gnelfdom of the forest gnelves is relying on us. May the power of the compass-clock and the wisdom of the elders be with all three of us." And with that, Sorrel vanished into the shadows of the cliff.

Matthew turned to Leo and said in a panic-stricken voice, "Leo, what are we doing? We can't fight the quokkerwodgers and the dark gnelves. They might use magic on us!"

"I know, I know," replied Leo, "but we can't go back now, and we have to help Sorrel if we can. You heard him. His whole gnelfdom is relying on us. Look, I suspect the quokkerwodgers are as small as he is, or smaller. We'll be like giants to them."

Matthew did not look totally convinced but he fell silent and he and Leo crouched together in the cave wall, waiting for their signal. They both wished that Rocket was with them, as she would certainly chase after a few dark gnelves. They didn't have to wait long. Out of the silence came the distant rhythmic noise of marching feet. Leo and Matthew leant forward to get a better view of the entrance to the Kolldor Caves. Suddenly, two gnelves appeared at the mouth of the cave. They were the same height and build as Sorrel, but their hats and their eyes were as black as the night sky. They each had a staff in their hands and a black ring on one of their fingers.

"Those must be dark gnelves," Leo whispered to Matthew.

The two dark gnelves stood at the cave entrance, one male and one female, and they looked around. After what seemed like a long time, they raised their staffs and pointed forward. They stepped out from the shadows of the cave and started to march in the direction of some trees in the distance. Behind the dark gnelves emerged creatures that Leo and Matthew had never seen before. They were small and squat with pointed ears and round potbellies. They had spiky indigo-coloured hair and tiny mushroom noses. They wore dark blue clothing and were the ugliest creatures that Leo and Matthew had ever seen.

"They must be the quokkerwodgers," whispered Leo.

They emerged in pairs, marching gloomily and rather reluctantly behind the two dark gnelves. Together, the dark gnelves and the quokkerwodgers formed a rather sinister and miserable procession.

After a few more pairs of quokkerwodgers had emerged out of the cave, suddenly there was a bit of a gap before four of them stepped out together. These four were carrying a wooden crate that had been tied to two poles, which was resting on the shoulders of the four quokkerwodgers. A green glow shone through the cracks of the crate and caught their attention. Whatever was inside the crate was clearly very important and it was what the dark gnelves and the quokkerwodgers were carefully protecting.

"That's it! That must be the Conifer Crown. Inside that crate!" whispered Matthew, but before Leo had a chance to answer there came a loud, long whistle from the other side of the cave. That was their signal from Sorrel.

10

Battle!

Leo and Matthew jumped up and charged out from their hiding place. They ran directly at the marching pairs, screaming as loudly as they could, waving their sticks angrily in the air. It was clear from the terrified look on their faces that the quokkerwodgers had no idea who or what they were. They all screeched and started to scatter. This gave Leo and Matthew the confidence they needed. They ran straight into the quokkerwodgers who were no taller than their knees, and with one swipe of their sticks they sent the quokkerwodgers soaring through the air and tumbling over the ground. The four quokkerwodgers carrying the crate dropped it in pure terror. The crate crashed to the ground, burst open and splintered into pieces. Out of the crate fell a glowing green object, and it rolled along the rocky ground. It was the Conifer Crown. The crown was carefully crafted from woven twigs and fir cones which glinted like glass. Leaves of all shapes and sizes filled the gaps and it gave out an emerald green light that lit the surrounding area. Leo could see why Devellza wanted it so badly; it was beautiful. The Conifer Crown rolled to a stop, glowing its emerald green colour amongst the broken planks of the crate. The two dark gnelves at the front jumped into action and immediately separated. One of them dashed straight back towards the cave to raise the alarm and to fetch reinforcements.

Sorrel had burst from his hiding place at the same time as Leo and Matthew. He had ducked between the panicked quokkerwodgers and had made a beeline for the broken crate. The dark gnelf who was left by herself had spotted Sorrel and saw what he was going to do. She picked up her staff and started running towards the Conifer Crown that lay unprotected on the ground. As Sorrel and the dark gnelf got closer to the Conifer Crown, they ignored it and ran straight at each other, coming together with an almighty crash. Their sticks banged together, and they wrestled together on the ground, tumbling over each other. They were hitting and kicking the other until one of them would use some ancient magic and suddenly disappear, leaving the other sprawled on the ground. Then they would reappear directly behind the other one and attack again.

By now, the quokkerwodgers had dispersed, but there was a lot of noise rumbling from the inside of the caves and it was getting louder. Reinforcements were on their way. Sorrel and the dark gnelf had taken little notice of the boys and suddenly they were fighting right next to where Leo stood. Leo was desperate to help and without thinking, bent forwards and grabbed the black hat off the top of the dark gnelf's head. Leo pulled it clean off and lifted it high above his own head. The dark gnelf squealed and spun around. She looked up in terror at Leo, she had never been so close to a human before, never mind touched by one. Leo threw the hat to the ground and Sorrel seized the opportunity. He raised his hands and pointed his wiggling fingers towards the dark gnelf as she ran to her hat. A ball of golden light appeared and hovered in front of his fingers. The dark gnelf had lost her focus and had not noticed what Sorrel was doing. With a decisive flick of his fingers, the golden ball of light flew from Sorrel's hands and hit the dark gnelf in the small of her back. She yelped in agony and was thrown to the ground. Now she looked scared and before anything else could happen the dark gnelf grabbed her staff and hat, and she staggered back towards the cave entrance in retreat. Sorrel looked exhausted from the effort it had taken. Creating the golden ball of light had taken all his strength but he managed to throw a quick smile at Leo.

Leo felt a rush of jubilation and knew they had won. He leapt in the air with delight, but his eyes were drawn upwards and he caught sight of something that suddenly made his blood run cold and it wiped the smile from his face. There, standing on a rocky outcrop from the cliff and lit in the eerie moonlight, was a solitary figure. It was a single female dark gnelf and the sight of her sent shivers straight through Leo. She wore black clothes and had a black cape, which had gold lining and gold edging. Her hair was jet black but had a streak of gold that ran down the left-hand side. Her eyes were the scariest eyes Leo had ever seen. Her right eye was dark and menacing like all dark gnelves, but her left eye was unlike any he had seen on a dark gnelf. It was a rich golden colour, but the way it stared at him was cruel and sinister. She stood like a statue, holding a golden staff. More than that though, both her eyes were locked directly onto Leo and he knew immediately that he was staring into the eyes of Devellza.

Leo screamed and pointed up at the figure. Sorrel and Matthew both looked up, and Matthew let out a shriek. There was no time to lose.

"It's Devellza! Quick, get the Conifer Crown! We've got to get out of here," shouted Sorrel.

Matthew, who was nearest the crown, grabbed it from the floor just as a stream of dark gnelves poured angrily from the entrance of the cave, like a swarm of locusts, screaming menacingly and waving sticks at the three of them. Leo, Matthew and Sorrel started to sprint towards the large, proud fir tree on the edge of the clearing. They all glanced up and saw that Devellza had disappeared from her spot on the ridge.

"Quick! Run! Back to the warrinth," shouted Sorrel. "To the Forest Gnelfdom."

As Leo ran, he glanced back over his shoulders and saw a swarm of angry dark gnelves rushing towards them. They were expressionless, with blank, ghostly looks on their faces, and with huge black eyes staring intensely at them. Their mouths were wide open, and they were screaming fiercely at the boys. Their black eyes never blinked, and they just kept staring, as if in a trance. Leo ran a little faster, they were nearly at the tree. Suddenly, there was a burst of movement in the branches of the fir tree and down the trunk ran a scurry of squirrel spies. They formed a huddle at the base of the tree, and to their horror, they blocked the entrance to the warrinth. Sorrel and the boys screeched to a halt. Quickly the dark gnelves caught up with them and formed a semi-circle around the three of them. The three of them had nowhere to go. There were squirrel spies in front of them and dark gnelves behind them. They were trapped.

"What do we do?" hissed Leo anxiously. "Sorrel, use your magic!" But Sorrel still looked tired from using his ball of golden light earlier.

"I'm not powerful enough to defeat all of them," he replied. "We must prepare to fight."

"But there are so many of them now," uttered Matthew in dismay, realising they no longer had the advantage of surprise.

The unflinching and menacing stares of the dark gnelves bore straight into the boys. Their lips were snarled at the corners and it was clear they were ready to fight. Without warning, the dark gnelves all slowly raised their staffs and pointed them directly at the two boys. They were about to attack. Leo and Matthew braced themselves for what was about to happen. Leo bitterly regretted putting himself and Matthew in this position. Would they ever get out of the forest alive? He knew he needed to find that inner strength, that confidence he knew he had. He had to be brave. He could do it. He would fight for himself, for Matthew, but above all he would fight for Sorrel. He would do it for justice and for what was right. Leo took a deep breath, stood tall and opened his eyes. He was ready. He locked eyes with one of the nearest dark gnelves and just as he was about to charge, a long piercing sound came from the entrance of the cave.

"HALT!" screamed a deep female voice. "Dark gnelves, back!" bellowed the same voice, and instantly the dark gnelves dropped their staffs and fell back to create an opening in the semi-circle. Out of the mouth of the caves, and coming directly towards them, strode their worst fear; the leader of the dark gnelves. It was Devellza!

11

Devellza

Devellza marched through the lines of dark gnelves and came straight up to Sorrel and the two boys. Her black and gold cloak billowed behind her and she was carrying a golden staff. She stopped in front of them and pointed directly at Matthew. They shrank back in fear, the different coloured eyes were terrifying.

"I think you have something of mine, human! You will give it back to me immediately." She reached out her empty hand towards Matthew. Leo noticed that one hand was like all the other dark gnelves, with gnarly fingers, grey skin and black fingernails. However, her left hand had long, pointed, slender fingers, and her skin was creamy and smooth, with a golden glint to it. Her fingernails were a golden colour that matched the golden streak in her hair and her golden eye. Leo found her very unnerving but also mesmerising.

Matthew looked helplessly at Sorrel, who solemnly nodded his head in consent. There was nothing Matthew could do other than reluctantly place the Conifer Crown into the open hand of Devellza. She turned around, raised the crown up above her head and all the dark gnelves cheered in celebration. She placed it carefully on her head and turned back to face them.

"The Conifer Crown is mine!" she started. "It will join the Crystal Crown and, with them together, my powers will grow stronger. Soon, all the crowns will be mine and then I shall rule over all the gnelfdoms and every gnelf will bow before me!" At this, all the dark gnelves started cheering once again.

"Silence!" screeched Devellza and the cheering stopped immediately. "Now, tell me," she said slowly, looking at Leo and Matthew, "Who are you? Why are you helping this pathetic forest gnelf?"

"I am not pathetic," shouted Sorrel. "That crown is ours. It belongs to the forest gnelves."

"Shut up! I don't want to hear any more from you!" snarled Devellza. "Guards, take the gnelf and put him in a locking toadstool. Soon, he will be one of us!" she cackled with glee. Two dark gnelves stepped forward and grabbed Sorrel by his shoulders, dragging him aside.

"No, wait!" shouted Leo, stepping forward, a little surprised at his own bravery. "You can't do this. He was only trying to get back what is rightfully his." Matthew grabbed Leo by his arm, warning him not to go too far. Devellza noticed the gesture.

"Your friend is right to restrain you." She said in her smooth, deep voice. "You should learn some respect, boy. Now, what am I going to do with you? Hmmm, you are both too big for a locking toadstool." Matthew glanced at Leo in alarm. Leo was very pleased he had grown a couple more centimetres in the last year. "Shame, I could have done with a couple of guards your size. Think of the advantage I would have in battle. Hmmm, maybe there's another way," she finished with a wicked grin.

"You wouldn't dare!" blurted Matthew. "Besides, we're humans. You can't turn us into dark gnelves!" He had spoken in confidence, but suddenly he had a feeling of doubt. Both boys looked at Sorrel for reassurance, but instead he just bowed his head in sorrow. Leo gulped.

"Aha! You have no idea of the powers that we gnelves can have. How do you think we have survived through the passage of time? This golden staff," and she held it up for all to see, "is forged from the same material as the compass-clock. They are connected and I can draw upon the powers of the Secretan." Devellza lifted her staff as if she were about to strike the boys. A hush fell over the dark gnelves and the squirrel spies retreated to the treeline.

Leo and Matthew knew she was not lying and suddenly they realised they were in mortal danger. Leo grabbed Matthew by the arm and looked into his eyes. He could see that Matthew was as scared as he was. He only had time to utter the words, "I'm sorry," before there was a loud BANG and a whizzing noise. Golden sparks flew through the air and the two boys braced themselves for the powerful bolt from Devellza's staff, but it never came.

Instead, a large ball of golden light flew out from the trees and hit Devellza square in the chest.

"Aaaaaaaaaaaah," she screamed as she was knocked off her feet. The Conifer Crown fell from her head and crashed to the ground. The boys looked up as the dark gnelves yelped and started to panic. The two gnelves holding Sorrel let go of him and backed away with the others. They turned to look at the forest and could not believe their eyes. A black and white blur tore through the bushes and then, out into the open burst Rocket, barking madly and baring her teeth. She ran directly at the terrified dark gnelves who started screaming and began running and cartwheeling in all directions. The squirrel spies scarpered up the trees and out of sight. Leo suddenly realised that Rocket was not alone. On her back rode another gnelf. This gnelf looked very similar to Sorrel, only he had an orange hat on instead. He had an orange ring on his finger, and he had bright orange eyes. He was holding onto Rocket's collar, guiding her towards the dark gnelves.

Sorrel exchanged an understanding look with the new gnelf and ran over to where Devellza lay sprawled on the ground. He grabbed the Conifer Crown and sprinted back to the boys. "Quick! Take this!" and he thrust the Conifer Crown into the hands of Leo. "You're stronger and taller than me. Hold it tight! Now, quickly, we must get into the warrinth!" It was the first time Leo had held the crown and it was heavier than he had imagined.

"But what about Rocket?" shouted Leo as he watched her racing around the open space with the gnelf on her back. As soon as Rocket got near a dark gnelf, it would drop to the ground and turn into a rock, much to her annoyance, and she would growl and bark at the rock before lurching after a new victim.

Devellza began to stir on the ground, which Sorrel noticed. "Don't worry, Rocket will be fine. Trust me! We have to go!" he said hastily.

As Sorrel and the boys turned towards the fir tree, which was now clear of squirrel spies, Devellza sat up and saw what was happening. She screeched at the top of her voice, "Quick! Stop them!" and the dark gnelves who were closest turned their attention to the three of them.

"RUN!" shouted Sorrel and they immediately all ran towards the tree. Leo hesitated, reluctant to leave Rocket, but he noticed that Rocket had stopped chasing the dark gnelves and was heading back into the forest. He had to trust Sorrel and hoped that she would be okay.

"After them!" bellowed Devellza, who was beginning to find her strength and had staggered to her feet. Leo could hear the dark gnelves running towards them. He tried to run faster.

Sorrel reached the tree first and ran straight into the warrinth, followed quickly by Matthew, who was wasting no time getting to safety. The dark gnelves were nearly upon them, their hands reaching forward, when finally, Leo dived into the tree still clutching the crown closely to his chest. The sowldier hooted each time one of them entered.

Leo realised he had been holding his breath, he gasped and breathed in the cold tunnel air and immediately felt safer. The vacuum of the warrinth took hold of Leo and as he hurtled down the passageway the Secretan's melodic voice asked him where he was going. In a moment of panic, Leo forgot what Sorrel had told them, then it suddenly came back to him, "The Forest Gnelfdom," he shouted. He could see Matthew up ahead, zipping along nicely, and Sorrel up ahead of him. Leo was so relieved to be leaving Devellza, the dark gnelves and the Kolldor Caves behind him. He dearly hoped Rocket would find her way through the forest.

However, something else didn't feel right and his instincts told him there was a problem. It dawned on Leo that the last thing that he had heard, among the screaming of the dark gnelves as he entered the warrinth, was a fourth hoot from the sowldier. With a sickening feeling of dread, Leo realised that someone or something had followed them into the warrinth.

12

A Helping Hand

Leo was desperate to speed up and get closer to Matthew, or try to tell Sorrel, but he realised that the vacuum felt slower this time. In fact, he was not catching Matthew up, the opposite was happening, Matthew was disappearing into the distance. He also felt heavier than usual, more sluggish. Leo looked back, and another cold shiver ran down his spine. To his horror he saw a pair of large black eyes staring straight at him. There was a dark gnelf holding onto his foot. He must have grabbed it when Leo had entered the warrinth. That was the fourth hoot. Leo shook his foot from side to side and tried desperately to shake the dark gnelf off, but the gnelf's grip only tightened. He tried and tried but nothing would work. The dark gnelf now had a hand on his ankle and was beginning to climb up his leg, his lips curling into a snarl. Leo tried to kick the dark gnelf with his other foot but the dark gnelf dodged each time. He tried to crash into the sides of the tunnel, but he remembered the warrinth was designed to not allow that to happen. The vacuum always pulled Leo back into the centre. No amount of thrashing about could dislodge the dark gnelf from his leg. The gnelf was now up to his thigh, those evil black eyes still staring straight at him. Leo began to panic, and he stretched the Conifer Crown out in front of him, as far away from the dark gnelf as possible.

Suddenly, from nowhere, there was an almighty whoosh of air and a streak of orange. Something slammed straight into the side of the dark gnelf. The dark gnelf yelped, lost his grip and tumbled away from Leo's leg. He watched as the dark gnelf veered off and flew down a different tunnel and disappeared out of sight. Leo let out a huge sigh of relief. He looked back and just had time to see the same streak of orange vanishing into another tunnel. What was it? What or who had helped him? Could it be the same gnelf that had appeared from the forest on Rocket's back? Surely not, but if it was, where was Rocket? Leo was eager to get the answers, but he had to concentrate on catching up with the others.

Leo focused on the tunnels ahead and it was not long before he was back in the mossy green tunnels leading to the Forest Gnelfdom and before he knew it, he was spat out of a tree. Matthew and Sorrel were standing there looking worried, but before Leo could say anything, he tripped and fell forward. He managed to somersault still holding onto the crown and ended up in a sitting position at Sorrel's feet.

"Ouch!" exclaimed Leo, "why can't I exit the warrinth properly?" He handed the Conifer Crown back to Sorrel for safe keeping.

Matthew helped Leo to his feet and Leo quickly explained what had happened to him in the warrinth, and his concerns about Rocket. Sorrel and Matthew listened intently.

"Gosh, I had no idea that was happening behind me, that sounds terrifying," said Matthew, with a worried look on his face, "but what was the orange streak that saved you?"

"I think I know," interrupted Sorrel, "but I'll explain later. Rocket is fine, I promise. We need to get the

Conifer Crown back into its rightful place. We need to keep moving."

"But why didn't Devellza stop us?" Leo wanted to know, "She could have used her staff and her powers!" There was also an element of relief in Leo's voice that she had not used them.

"She has never seen humans and gnelves interacting before. She was assessing your powers. That zappol took her by surprise." Sorrel replied glancing around. "We're not safe yet. Hurry! Follow me." He turned around and headed into the bushes.

"A zap what?" said Matthew to Leo, who could only shrug in reply and follow Sorrel into the bushes. The three of them crept through the forest until at last Sorrel seemed a little more relaxed. He paused and sat on a tree trunk to let Leo and Matthew catch up.

"We're nearly there!" he said with relief, as the boys caught up with him. "Let's keep going."

"Wait," Matthew stopped him, "before we go, I need to know something."

"What is it?" asked Sorrel.

"Why didn't the dark gnelves use their magic on us, the same way you did on that dark gnelf?" asked Matthew.

"You saw how much energy it took to create our magic weapon; a zappol, that ball of light," explained Sorrel. "It took all my strength because the Conifer Crown was not here, not in its rightful place. Therefore, my powers were limited. The dark gnelves cannot create zappols without life-sources. That is why they stole ours and why they need more. The life-sources are never as powerful out of their gnelfdoms but that is why Devellza wants them all for herself."

"Wow, I wish I could create a zappol," admired Matthew.

"Zappols are not to be played with Mr. Matthew," Sorrel continued. "If they strike you, it's like being struck by lightning. A zappol is a ball of natural electricity that stuns you and immediately makes you defenceless. They can be very powerful. It was a zappol that hit Devellza in the chest and stopped her from harming you."

Leo was listening intently but there was something else playing on his mind, "Sorrel, can I ask a question too? Who was the gnelf on Rocket's back? And you haven't told us what that orange streak was that saved me from the dark gnelf in the warrinth? Mind you, we still don't even know if Rocket is okay! I really want to get her back."

"Ah yes! Come with me," and Sorrel led the boys to a spot where four trees grew close together and intertwined. "This is our meeting spot." He lifted his hand into the air and blew on his sensor-ring. Immediately, there was a rustling to the side and out of the ferns stepped another gnelf. It was the same gnelf with an orange hat that had ridden Rocket and his bright orange eyes danced like flames. Leo noticed he was holding Rocket's lead and then out into the clearing stepped Rocket too.

"Rocket!" shouted both the boys in unison. Rocket saw them and immediately bounded over, wagging her tail and jumping up to lick Leo's face. Leo and Matthew both knelt and gave her an almighty hug. They were so relieved to see her.

"This is Blaze," introduced Sorrel. He is a fire gnelf and a protector of gnelves. Fire gnelves roam freely like the dark gnelves and they help any gnelf in need. Fire gnelves only approach you if you summon them or they sense you are in danger. If you blow onto your sensor-ring a fire gnelf will always come to your aid. They bring light to the darkness. Blaze and I are old friends."

Leo stepped forward, "It's a pleasure to finally meet you, Blaze. My name is Leo, and this is Matthew. You have been watching us, haven't you? You were there when we saved Sorrel from the locking toadstool and you followed us through the forest."

"You are right, Mr. Leo," Blaze answered warmly, "and it is nice to meet you too. Locking toadstools are deadly poisonous for fire gnelves, cursed by Devellza's dark magic, but you, as humans, were unaffected by it and you were able to save Sorrel. I am very grateful that you saved my friend."

Sorrel added, "I suspect that's why Devellza didn't attack you straight away when she had us trapped. She realised the toadstool magic had not worked on you and she was being cautious."

Blaze continued, "Any rescuer of Sorrel is a friend of mine. I have been watching you from a distance as I thought you might need my help at some point. I watched you leave Rocket at the entrance to the warrinth, so I took her with me, in case we could be of any assistance. Dogs are used to running over great distances, so we didn't need to use the warrinth. I wanted to make sure you could return home safely, like Sorrel can. Luckily, all the squirrel spies were busy guarding the entrance to the warrinth, when you were trapped, so they didn't notice Rocket and me approaching." Blaze finished with a grin.

Leo smiled back, "Yes, you're right, that was lucky! Thank goodness! Well, I also need to thank you for saving me from the dark gnelf in the warrinth. That was very scary, and I am very grateful."

Blaze let out a chuckle, "That was not me, Mr. Leo, I was racing back through the forest with Rocket. That was another fire gnelf. I asked her to keep an eye on you in the warrinth." Blaze held up his hand and blew on his sensor-ring. A moment later there was a rustle to the side and into the clearing stepped another fire gnelf. She had orange eyes, like Blaze, pretty eyelashes and rosy cheeks. She certainly didn't look like the angry orange streak that Leo had seen in the warrinth. "This is Ember, my apprentice," said Blaze.

Ember smiled, "It's a pleasure to meet you both. I'm glad I was able to help you in the warrinth."

"Thank you so much," said Leo gratefully, "I'm not sure how to repay you."

"Fire gnelves do not need repayment," Ember said reassuringly. "It is our responsibility to help protect all the gnelves and all the different gnelfdoms. You may not be gnelves, but you were helping Sorrel and the forest gnelves. I was only doing my duty."

"It is a great honour to become a fire gnelf," Sorrel explained. "Each year the Gnelflethic Games are held, where gnelves are selected from all the different gnelfdoms to compete against one another to win the title of Fire Victor. The winning gnelf extinguishes the ceremonial flame, absorbing its power and taking up a new position as a fire gnelf."

"Wow, that sounds amazing! You don't get anything like that when you win sports day at school!" Matthew said with a sense of awe.

Leo grinned at Matthew's comment, but Sorrel continued, "Every new fire gnelf becomes an apprentice to another. Their life-source is heat and light, so they often sit in the sun. Their zappols are more powerful than the average gnelf's, like the one you saw Blaze use against Devellza. Fire gnelves are highly trained and take a vow to help protect all gnelfdoms."

Blaze could see how impressed the boys were. "Maybe one day you can come and watch the Gnelfletic Games for yourselves," suggested Blaze.

"Wow, we would love that, if it were ever possible! So, does that mean we will see you both again?" Leo asked Blaze and Ember, with an increased sense of respect and admiration for the fire gnelves.

Blaze and Ember looked at each other and smiled. "Yes, Mr. Leo. We will see you and Mr. Matthew again," replied Blaze. "There are many gnelfdoms out there, and there is always one that will need your help. News will spread about what you two have done for the forest gnelves. I have no doubt that other gnelves may seek your help and we will always be there to help too. I am certain that Devellza will want to see you again. She will no doubt want her revenge."

Leo and Matthew were alarmed at what Blaze had said and looked at each other in horror, but Ember saw their concern and said with a comforting smile, "Don't worry, we will always be watching."

Before they could ask anything else, Blaze and Ember vanished into the forest, in another streak of orange. Rocket let out a startled bark, but quickly the bushes were still again.

"Come on, we need to get home," said Sorrel, seemingly unsurprised by the sudden departure of his friends.

13

New Friends

Sorrel led Leo and Matthew through more ferns and brambles until they came upon another small clearing. On the other side of the clearing was an arch of ferns between two rhododendron bushes and there was some noise beyond it. Sorrel walked straight up to the archway and beckoned to the boys to follow him. Rocket trotted after Sorrel.

Leo and Matthew had to crouch down to walk through the archway. They found themselves in a large, deserted enclave with a few solitary trees standing lonely and still, and a few rocks and ferns scattered about. Rhododendron bushes ran all the way around the edge.

"This is the heart of our gnelfdom, welcome to our home!" announced Sorrel proudly.

The two boys looked closer and there were some withered old mushrooms that lined the edges of the clearing and damp pinecones hung from the branches above. There were some drooping vines hanging down from the trees and a few mossy rocks scattered around the clearing. It was empty of any life or colour and they felt it was not anything very special. Leo and Matthew were not sure what to say.

"It's okay, they're with me! Come out everyone! We have the Conifer Crown!" shouted Sorrel with a huge grin on his face.

With his announcement everything changed. Pieces of bark were pushed open from inside the trees to reveal tiny windows. The pinecones unfurled into tiny lamps, the mushrooms stood upright and beautiful flowers blossomed on the rhododendron bushes. Ferns and brambles picked themselves off the ground helping form protective walls around the clearing and daisies and crocuses sprung up in the grass. The rocks started to quiver and uncurl themselves, forest gnelves began to stand up all around the clearing. Some were taller than others, there were young ones and older ones. The male gnelves often had long beards and the female gnelves all had rosy cheeks and pretty faces. However, there were three things they all had in common: their bright green eyes, the emerald green sensor-rings on their fingers and their bottle-green gnelf hats.

The forest gnelves all stood and stared apprehensively and inquisitively at Leo and Matthew. Then they noticed what Sorrel was holding. It was indeed their beloved life-source, the Conifer Crown. It was back and it glowed magnificently in Sorrel's hands. There were cries of delight and the forest gnelves started calling to friends and neighbours to come and see. More and more forest gnelves ran into the clearing, some even cartwheeled, until there were excited gasps and chatter all around them. The boys were astonished at what they were witnessing and the gnelves crowded round, giving Rocket some comforting pats too, who wagged her tail in delight. One gnelf with short, wavy hair and long eyelashes came and put her arms around Sorrel and gave him a big kiss on his cheek.

Sorrel turned to the boys and said, "Mr. Leo and Mr. Matthew, I want you to meet my soulmate, Teak."

Leo and Matthew said hello to Teak and then they started being introduced to all of Sorrel and Teak's friends and many more of the forest gnelves. They all wanted to see the Conifer Crown for themselves. After a minute or two, a sudden hush descended on the gathered gnelves and they stepped aside to create a parting through the middle. Leo and Matthew looked up and saw an elderly female gnelf walking towards them. She was beautiful, with long, white hair and flowing green robes. Her eyes were a deep, ancient-green colour and she looked very wise. She stopped just in front of them and looked up at their faces.

Sorrel stepped forward, "Aurora, we have returned, and we have brought the Conifer Crown with us." There was a cheer from the crowd and then Sorrel continued, "Mr. Leo and Mr. Matthew, may I introduce you to Aurora, the Conifer of our gnelfdom. She is the eldest and wisest forest gnelf. She is our leader." Sorrel paused and turned to his leader, "Aurora, these are the two human warriors that I told you about. They have shown bravery beyond their years and helped me return the Conifer Crown to our gnelfdom."

"Your Royal Coniferness," blurted Leo, "it's a pleasure to meet you."

The forest gnelves sniggered, and Leo tried to cover his blushing cheeks.

"Quiet!" ordered the Conifer and then she addressed Leo and Matthew directly, "Please ignore them. They have forgotten their manners. I am enchanted to meet you both, but please, call me Aurora. We do not use titles here. This is a very special day for us; not only do we meet humankind, but you return our most prized possession to us; the Conifer Crown. This crown is our life-source and gives power to the nature around us and strengthens our magic too. We will need it to help defend ourselves from Devellza and the dark gnelves. Thank you, for returning it to us."

The Conifer held out her hands. Sorrel smiled, passing the Conifer Crown to Leo and Matthew who, together, had the honour of placing it into Aurora's hands. There were cheers from all around them.

"Thank you," said the Conifer, "the forest gnelves will be forever grateful for your assistance and in return I would like to present you both with a token of our appreciation. Come! The presentation will take place immediately."

Leo and Matthew were led through the clearing to a ring of colourful toadstools that they were invited to sit on. The forest gnelves gathered around excitedly. Sorrel and Teak sat opposite Leo and Matthew, and the Conifer sat on the tallest toadstool with the members of her council on either side. When the Conifer stood up, the crowd fell silent. She lifted the Conifer Crown up for all of them to see and placed it in its rightful place, in a hollow in the tree above her. Immediately, it shone brighter, and a surge of energy rippled through the tree, down to its roots and out across the clearing. The flowers stood up straight, the pinecone lanterns suddenly shone brighter and the forest gnelves all cheered heartily.

"My dear forest gnelves, let me begin by saying what a very special day this is, and how lucky we are to have the Conifer Crown returned to us. Without the help of these human boys and their wonderful dog Rocket, it would never have been possible. Leo and Matthew," started the Conifer, "on behalf of all forest gnelves and from the powers of the compass-clock I would like to present you both with one of the most prized treasures that any gnelf may own; a sensor-ring." There were gasps from the crowd. No human had ever been rewarded with such an honour before. The Conifer continued, "Now that you have been exposed to the darkness in our lands, these rings will help protect you. If you ever feel them vibrate on your finger, then move away from the shadows. Devellza and the dark gnelves cannot be seen by other humans, but they can still play mean tricks on you. Twist the ring and it will let out an ear-piercing noise that will send them running from you. Guard the rings carefully. They will not be replaced."

Leo and Matthew stepped forward one at a time to receive the sensor-rings, thanking Aurora as they did so. Each was received by a rapturous round of applause.

"Leo and Matthew, you will always be welcome in the Gnelfdom of Forest Gnelves and you will always find a home here. Finally, we have a wreath of gratitude to present to our brave animal-friend; Rocket." Teak stepped forward to place a beautiful wreath of forest flowers over Rocket's head, and she wagged her tail happily.

"This concludes the ceremony. Let the celebrations begin!" announced the Conifer and there was more rapturous applause around the clearing.

14

Promises

All the gnelves busied themselves setting up for a special celebration. They were happy that all their morning chores were on hold. A party was much more fun. Some put up gold and green bunting, others laid out some fizzy drinks and the rest were hanging amber balloons, which Sorrel explained had been blown from the sap of trees. The return of the Conifer Crown had created an excited buzz in the air. Then the party began. Music played and the gnelves chatted and danced in the clearing. Whilst the boys watched the gnelves enjoying themselves, Sorrel came and sat beside Leo and Matthew.

"Mr. Leo and Mr. Matthew," started Sorrel, but Matthew interrupted him.

"Hang on," Matthew said, "didn't Aurora say there were no titles here. You can stop saying 'Mr' now."

The three of them smiled and laughed together. "Okay, you're right... Leo and Matthew," said Sorrel tentatively, "I think it is time we returned you to where you belong."

Leo and Matthew realised that the morning sun was climbing higher in the sky and if they didn't turn up for breakfast soon, then Leo's parents would come looking for them. They also realised that they had been up all night and had not slept. Tiredness began to sweep over them.

"Maybe you're right," said Leo, "but I don't really want to leave."

"Me neither," agreed Matthew, "this has been the best night of my life! Let's stay a few more minutes. Sorrel, you have taught us so much and I'm sure I could think of lots more questions for you, but there is one I want to ask."

"I will always try to answer any question that you have. What is it?" asked Sorrel.

Matthew hesitated before asking, "Why is Devellza so powerful? Is it because she has those gold bits on her?"

"Hmmm, that is a good question, Matthew," began Sorrel. "No one knows for sure, but rumour has it that Devellza was once a gnelf like us but also greedy for power. One day, she tried to take control of the compass-clock, to strengthen her abilities. However, she underestimated its true power, and when she touched it, she received a zappol so great that it sent a golden bolt of electricity through her entire body. They say it was the zappol that streaked the gold through the left-hand side of her body. She nearly died, but the Secretan put her into a locking toadstool as punishment. You see, dark gnelves were nothing back then. However, there was residue of the zappol left in her, which meant that when she came out of the toadstool, she wasn't an ordinary dark gnelf, she had become the powerful dark gnelf that we know today. Other dark gnelves realised they finally had someone who they could follow, so word spread and she quickly gathered many around her. Soon afterwards, they attacked the Kolldor Caves and... well, the rest you already know."

"Gosh, she really does sound like a nightmare," said Matthew. He and Leo were both glad they had not known all this before they saw her high up on the ridge.

"Come, we must leave now," said Sorrel. "Devellza will be sending out squirrel spies to find you. Now she knows how to use you, she will want to catch you. Promise me that you will stay away from any forests for a while."

Leo and Matthew thought that was an excellent plan. "We promise!" they said in unison. There would be no more forests for the foreseeable future.

They went back and said goodbye to Teak and to Aurora and to collect Rocket. She was enjoying all the attention but grudgingly trotted off alongside Leo and Matthew. As the three of them left the forest gnelfdom with Sorrel by their side, they turned and waved goodbye to all the forest gnelves, who all waved back and cheered enthusiastically.

Sorrel led them back through the brambles and ferns. It was easier now with the rising sun and as they approached the warrinth tree, Sorrel turned to the boys, "This is where I must leave you. Ask the warrinth for Cosy Nook Beach, it's only a short journey from here. I will ride Rocket there myself. Wait for her on the beach. Promise me that you will keep those rings and hats safe and that you'll show them to no one!"

"We promise!" said the boys again in unison, they could see how important it was to Sorrel.

"Good! Now, get home safely," Sorrel continued, "and promise to come and find us again!" He smiled warmly at them. "Thank you again for all you have done for us."

"No, it's us who must thank you, Sorrel. Of course we will find you again," said Leo, as he and Matthew watched as Sorrel jumped onto Rocket's back.

"Goodbye, Leo and Matthew, it has been an honour to have you by my side. Until we meet again!" He leant forward and whispered in Rocket's ear, who lurched forward, and they bounded into the ferns and brambles. The boys watched them disappear between the trees before turning to face each other.

"Wow, Matthew, is this real? Did all that really just happen? To us?" asked Leo.

"Yeah, I think it really did," replied Matthew, his eyes shining, "but let's go! We've got to get out of the forest before a squirrel spy sees us. I'm going first this time." He pulled his hat down securely on his head, took a deep breath and ran straight at the tree. With a hoot from the sowldier Matthew disappeared into the warrinth.

Leo also took a deep breath; he was not as confident about using the warrinth without Sorrel, but he knew he didn't have a choice. He lurched forward and ran straight at the tree. He had just enough time to hear the sowldier hoot before he plunged into the tree and found himself inside the magical tunnels once again.

This time, the journey through the warrinth was much shorter and the two boys really felt they were getting the hang of flying through the tunnels. It was not long before Leo and Matthew were spat out at the oak tree near Cosy Nook Beach. Matthew landed on his feet as usual and skidded to a stop. Leo thought he had mastered it, but once again was unable to stay upright and fell flat on his face, much to his annoyance.

"You'll get the hang of it one day," offered Matthew kindly, holding his hand out to Leo.

"I hope so," said Leo pulling himself up with Matthew's help and the two boys dashed through the forest, out to the shore and onto the beach. They pulled their gnelf hats off and stuffed them into their pockets along with their sensor-rings to keep them safe. Suddenly there was a rustling in the bushes behind them and the boys turned around in panic, dreading what they might see, but out jumped Rocket, very pleased to see them once again and wagging her tail ferociously. She had lost her wreath of flowers. Maybe Sorrel had taken it off her. Leo noticed another flash of orange in the bushes, but this time he knew what it was, and he knew that Sorrel and Rocket had been protected through the forest. He smiled gratefully.

The two boys and Rocket ran along the beach, made their way up the mossy path, picked up their sleeping bags from under the bush and ran through the rickety gate. Just as they arrived at their pitch, Leo's parents stepped out from the tent with relieved looks on their faces.

"Where have you been?" asked Leo's father anxiously. "We were about to come and look for you! Why didn't you reply to my messages?"

Leo had forgotten he had his mum's phone. "Oh sorry, I didn't turn it on. We were fine. We've been camping in our den, in the forest," replied Leo, trying to sound relaxed and casual about it, "like we said we were, and it didn't rain!"

"Can me and Rosalia come and see your den?" Issy asked excitedly, and quite innocently.

"Rosalia and I!" interrupted Mrs. Dickens, who was a stickler for grammar.

"Err no," Leo said, desperately trying to think of a reason why.

"We decided to take it down and leave the forest as we found it," helped Matthew hastily. "That's why we're a bit late. Remember; 'take only memories and leave only footprints.'"

"Yeah exactly, you know that Issy!" scoffed Leo, throwing a side glance to Matthew who was trying not to laugh. "Are we late for breakfast, Mum?" Leo said cheerfully, changing the topic. Issy did not look impressed, but she knew it was pointless complaining.

Leo's mother looked at the two boys and smiled, "See dear," she said turning to Leo's father, "I told you they were fine. Come on boys, the bacon is nearly ready, and I need my phone back please!"

"Gosh, look at Rocket," exclaimed Mr. Dickens, who was pointing to where Rocket had fallen asleep in the sunshine, "she looks exhausted. Anyone would have thought she had been running all night."

Leo nearly choked on the toast he was munching. "Well, she did chase a couple of squirrels," he said quite honestly, and then threw another grin at Matthew.

As the four of them munched their way through bacon rolls, Leo and Matthew were both very quiet. They were utterly exhausted, but they could not stop thinking about what they had been through. They thought about how much they had seen and had been told. They had discovered a whole new world that most humans never see. They had learnt about the different gnelfdoms, all the different types of gnelves, especially the forest gnelves who were now their friends. The squirrel spies, the sowldiers, the amazing warrinth and the compass-clock. Who was the Secretan? How far did the warrinth go? There was so much to discuss, but that would have to wait until they had caught up with their sleep.

One thing was for certain, both boys knew that they wanted to get back to the gnelf world again, to see Sorrel, Teak, Aurora, Blaze and Ember as soon as possible. In their tiredness the boys forgot Sorrel's final warning to them about forests and Leo turned to his mother with a glint in his eyes.

"Mum, when we get home, can I go to Matthew's house? Please!" Leo turned to Matthew, who was nodding in agreement, and Leo whispered excitedly to him, "Let's go and explore Muddletree Forest!"

The End